Violin Playing Herself in a Mirror

# Violin Playing Herself in a Mirror

*poems*

David Kutz-Marks

University of Massachusetts Press   *Amherst and Boston*

ISBN 978-1-62534-148-8

Designed by Sally Nichols
Set in ITC New Baskerville
Printed and bound by Maple Press Inc.


Library of Congress Cataloging-in-Publication Data

Kutz-Marks, David.
 [Poems. Selections]
 Violin playing herself in a mirror : poems / David Kutz-Marks.
    pages cm
 ISBN 978-1-62534-148-8 (pbk. : alk. paper)
 I. Title.
 PS3611.U89A6 2015
 811'.6–dc23
                                        2014050154


British Library Cataloguing-in-Publication Data
A catalogue record for this book is available from the British Library.

*For Arcadia and Lucas*

# Contents

# Acknowledgments

Grateful acknowledgement is made to the following journals, in which certain poems first appeared: *The 2River View:* "Fête"; *Another Chicago Magazine:* "Scene with Sheet Lightning"; *Boston Review:* "Curves and Intimations of a Great Disease"; *Caketrain:* "Gressorial Waltz"; *Cimarron Review:* "Cycle of a Scythe through a Field"; *Devil's Lake:* "Day on Which One Cycle Ends and One Begins" and "Recent Apparitions of Saturn"; *Greensboro Review:* "Meaning in Other Words"; *Kenyon Review Online:* "Two Lungs"; *Meridian:* "Najdorf Variations" and "A Thing on a Wall"; and *The Paris-American:* "Violin Playing Herself in a Mirror."

I also wish to thank Ben Myers and Marie Thurmer for all of their advice on the poems in this book; and my greatest teachers, Richard Howard, Srikanth Reddy, Sherry Ransford-Ramsdell, Timothy Donnelly, Mark Strand, Lucie Brock-Broido, Marjorie Welish, Campbell McGrath, and Eamon Grennan, for their brilliant teaching and encouragement; and most of all Rebecca Kutz-Marks, Charles Kutz-Marks, Marshall Kutz, Christine Olick, Arcadia Kutz-Marks, and Lucas Kutz-Marks, without whom this book would never have been written.

Violin Playing Herself in a Mirror

I

## Day on Which One Cycle Ends and One Begins

All the fireworkers on the third floor
couldn't put back together again your head, your ethereal car.

That was the essence of water, mulling you over and over and drifting off thoughtlessly,
then a century passes and a second ship

makes a puppet show of the horizon for a very long time.
Begging your pardon, the alcoholic simply didn't drink enough before he got on

and where did you think you were going
watching the skirts of the water ballet like a dog in a painting

the curtains never end, hanging at the edges of your vision
like leotards the gods have outgrown—meaningless

except that it was better, you thought, to have a wife and kids
and storm off to scar all the islands in some sort of circle

sleeping with a witch and then a saint and then a witch in the shape of a god.
You'd bronze up your body so hard

even the hydras, climbing up out of the Lethe and trying to block out the day,
would wince when they hit you.

Maybe you were never really lit at night.
Anyway, you just couldn't do it. It just wasn't you.

## Recent Apparitions of Saturn

All the Episcopal swimmers, fluting their bodies and fluting their hands—
new moon and crescent and gibbous and full, gibbous and crescent and new

nobody cares where your head may have been in the city, desisting,
everything about him is outsized, as somebody said,

and even his transcendent little body is transcended by the size and the glow
    of his hands,
he breaks walls with everything, with everything hopeless—he turns it around

in the eye of a horse on the quilt, which covers the door, and parts now and then,
revealing a child, growing up into a car.

The tectonic shifts that created the system, the little white backlit stars,
don't mean the mayor will sit down to dinner with us once we're done

trimming the hulls of the hedges—the Molotov cocktails are lit, the cocktails are sipped
in the front room of the passive old position of the world, which fits into a top
    hat, a rabbit

into the back of a truck, into the air on the farmland, into the town, hedged against
the city with the demon-red lights of the airport, which guide your father home.

So the wishbone is broken, but no one knows which of you won. Someone had mistaken
the brandy for a weak little thing, and slowly she finished the bottle

and spun through the rooms, eating the turkey and eating the pie
and the thistle said things, picking the food from his teeth, of a theory of life

or golden boughs and priest-kings, the big Caledonian ones,
but now as it stands, you're brushing your hair with your hand as you walk

and every third lot or so is vacant, and here you wish that you did not live.
Beverly's a damn good name, and Kevin and Tom,

and so the curtains parted with applause, and your daughter starts your car and sits
    and smokes,
and the horse ran off, having just been born.

# The Importance of Consistency in Discipline

Who the hell cares who the dark lady is?
It's a vivid line of reason from the hand into the mind

but the mystery here is better, leaving all the details of her face
back in the air as it were as you stare at the picture

riddled with hundreds of girders ascending each other
toward a prescribed position in the sky, and dutifully

the young man burned the blueprint long before this transpired.
Was he a lover? Was there a bird in his head?

These are only questions and he hastens to remind you that
she hastens to remind you that the water must be freezing

in the freezer—once again you've left your water in the freezer—
nothing like the village of this, nothing like the village of that,

though all the clap and the clapboard are fitted to match
how things were then, in the mind of the latest surveyor of things

with his hand on his hat and his hand on the hazel
prodding the earth here and there like a metal detector without any need

for what the earth has brought us since, or where the kites have gone,
eventually attaining all the shape and myth of dragons

and alien spacecraft and so on, a chime in the mind of a child,
a gong in the mind of an old and sad man with his hand on his hat

and his hand on the hazel, stirring the earth in his coffee,
taking a sip of his coffee, reading the paper, putting it down.

## The Couple in the Starry Night over the Rhone

What were you thinking, white as you were,
holding the hand of the half-gone man, under the water or over the water,

under the water you could not have been quite so white,
and the curve of the city above was the curve of your body

or out in the distance, neither above nor below where you were
but situated there, at the edge of what you're thinking

which has little to do with the starry night over the Rhone—
you had your own problems, how your five children

hated the half-gone man, and how you yourself, half-gone yourself,
wanted yourself to come down to the absence of color he had—

he was a model of that sort of thing, half in the world, and half in the cave,
man with a kite in his hand with the string in his hand

and the kite in the world, walking along in the world there beside you,
the starry night over the Rhone, the curve of the city, the curve of your body

fired by the stars in competition with the ever-growing lights of the city,
a feeling we extinguish and we put back on again.

## Najdorf Variations

No, nor do I want to.
There does remain however some glow in her hair

the wheat of the wheat in the sun
or, in the moon, the steel of the threshers.

She put her hurt behind her, a mirror time to time
she glimpsed in the corner.

It was the *fin de siècle* but not that one.
Therefore the icicles hummed from the ceiling,
the chandelier swung without light.

Dear you are gorgeous, but put on the necklace.
*Haven't I told you enough what it means?*
*This is the end, but here comes another.*

## Modern Greek and Cypriot Songs

The distance from the southern to the northern nurseries
was all in how you saw it, how the children would emerge

with violets in their hands, and violet in their hands,
and you thought it was better to think that no malice came of it (your changing yourself)

and you wandered back into the city by way of the church
via the roadway, via the sign for the vacant old town.

Naming yourself, putting the black little dress and the black little makeup
where women do, made you more like what

you wanted us to say you were, but nothing stopped the feeling of discovering
a Pocono Dome off the edge of the highway—

I never know what's happening in there—
or an indoor tennis court, Forest Hills for instance, pops up suddenly

and you try to get born, even though no mother will have you,
every sister marking up her door with all the same strange signs

meant to ward you off, and serving no other purpose,
purposeful enough that you would think that men would think

coming back home from a day at the factory, it would deter you—
No, you demurred, then we were immured within the same dome,

you loved the way the water on the stones was gold then black
then back to gold, and so for my part I admired

how the concertina wire would sing without reason,
wrapping the prison, as my two grown children made puzzles of light.

The town is full of parking signs, but no one seems to listen—
wearing her headlight, she started spelunking down into herself once again

and you never really know what she is looking for in there
but she seems to have a purpose.

Winter, and the evergreens stood tall against the edge
of the deciduous forest, knowing no humility—you stood among the
     evergreens and winter,

a big deer scattered on the road—how it comes and it goes, as he says,
and everyone cheers as he says it, just out of politeness,

and measuring the origin myths, against the little shadow of the eschatologies,
you realize for the first time that your son is taller

and your daughter is much taller than their mother,
who has shrunk a bit in the time since you last cared to measure her.

Right enough. She does the same thing—her eye is on the wing
of some bird out the window always.

She sits down to dinner only after you have eaten.
You put the heavy bones between your teeth.

He separates the faithful from the heathens—at least they have a purpose here,
he mutters in your ear, but you aren't quite sure which ones he means.

Old Deuteronomy says, God is my heart or my conscience,
I catch and kill birds and get fat for the winter and stand on a ladder and sing.

You swing back north along the highway crossing
for authorized personnel only, puffing on your little whitish stick.

Or you stand upon the myths, and stop somewhere amidst
the eschatologies, in other words the earth and the sky, but a very low one

underneath and no doubt offending some others.
Your brother is troubled, but no one has told him,

he lives at the edge of a dream and says stop like a clock,
you hear him though you have no use for time—that is what the thought is,

a sort of repurposed old vision you call from the back of the mind.
Are you tired? *I'm tired.* The city is happy to see you,

the grandfather flaunts his own shadow and enters the clock,
indigo buntings of indigo buntings have filled up the sky,

the little soup has earth in it and bread beside it.
You don't really mind but she does

and whether you see it or not, the basement is flooding—
your mother soothes herself beside the clock:

once Jack ascended the beanstalk Rapunzel let down her long hair,
a gold waterfall falling over a mountain, and once the man

was shipwrecked they tied him back down.
But by the time the tree became a man, the children had been whited back out into
    the scenery.

Or once the ancient men escaped the eye,
every night they slept against the rocks of that wall they remembered.

Or once the god dismembered all the ancient constellations, stars began to dim—
some died out, some went dormant, until

new constellations were formed, with the same stupid origins and names,
translated into new and degenerate languages.

The Amishman remembers almost no High German.
Nonetheless you carry on a conversation.

## Dementia Praecox

Not the *ding an sich,* but the *orange dinghy* we arrived in
nursing the wounded one back into whatever hell
the trip had created in us, Bobby with his flamethrower hair,
Penny with her caustic wit

and now and then a glimmer of a structure would give power
to our faces, or a drunk old statue.
It means, essentially, cleaving coming in and cans revolving,
etc., *I think in every ocean is a revolution,* as he says,

no one sure he's not just *saying it*
or where the thought is coming from, the tongue on the water
where we rest or just another of the *shiverers*
blurred like an island and strung out without clear purpose.

## Pressing the Advantage, Unaware of What It Was

Everyone studied in history. It was hard to say goodbye. All the maples as they were, just as you wanted, held out their red leaves like change, every field crisscrossed with parachute balls like the glass lightning globes in the cellar. You felt rejuvenated when the javelins happened to fly. Everyone studied in history. Slowly he took off the mortarboard and black juvenilia. In other words goodbye, but not before you set a foot in someone else's room, a straddling becoming a turn. Whether the horns can occur on the female and reach to the limb is another good question. Then there's the bird at the door who won't call what he's singing a song, or technically a warble, preferring just to sing it.

# Now I Am Ready to Troll the Big Lake

Ultimately then you had to have a mean dog,
with canines like stalactites in the foreground of the picture

backlit by the bluish white illusion of a wall.
Then you could just go on talking strung out

like a little mortal coil moonlighting as a halo
trying to eat his own tail in a city with no other light.

Vicious but not without reason the tithe
falls into the gold-rimmed lake of fire—folk songs are played

and you start to think you'll stay here awhile
like a child at a general store discovered off the highway

with the right kind of kitsch.
But the whole thing is vapid and fragile, a small shadow says,

and in some sense he means it—
your father, I mean, when he speaks of his father

or finishing dinner, sometimes both at once,
but you will have to go and kill the chicken with the hatchet

as we wait here at the table, and maple sap
becomes the spitting image of the viscous caramel candy of years

as first they take away the faceless table where
you want to sit and then the chicken gets away repeatedly

and your grandfather is back where you left him
telling his stories and making the salad

as the whole illicit store is closed, the front of it, the soul,
you had to have a mean dog in the corner

guarding the little trapdoor to the cellar
through which the light of the world came in lines

outlining a door where you stood turning vintage
on vintage, feeling old and liminal

backlit by the Edison bulbs that she ordered by mail-order catalog—
not the real ones from a century before

but painful imitations which consumed even more of your power
without real permission, with the same size and shape,

as the roar of the party above dragged the evening
back into the morning, with the roar of carousels bearing children.

II

## Eastern Queens

Another way of lowering a hand into a field
       eventually we realized she was painting our picture.

Whenever the clock in the cage struck a number
it chimed and she chirped, but not without a sort of resignation.

The spring yawns and tenses,
alternately breathing out the flowers through the nose

and holding its breath, as if there were something despondent to say,
too many heads in the picture

blocking the lamps, ruining the *mise-en-scène*.
       Then we went back to the cage

and ended our day with the wine and the bread—
what happens in cages does not pass the time as we'd like

but at least she puts a name to it and colors it in,
raising a hand to her face like she's fainting.

## Kimberly Wall

All these songs are the same,
it's hard to even know who's saying what, he says,

it is pain, the salve for which is nameless staring
into the womb hum.

I told her of my blanker adoration
just as a star crossed herself in a charcoal sketch

of where we were or are,
it's hard to really know a thing like this, he says,

producing a brown pipe and lighting the room,
plumes of it wriggling now through the air

without referent or anchor,
her hair I suppose, and the room is the world

where the man like an unwilling god
smokes and hums, and she walks a little fitfully.

## Five Narcissi Zeta-Tazetta

When, after six long years, the little man came back again
wearing his fedora we did not know what to say to him—

all the inconsistencies of things surrounded us again
(the goldfish in the bowl, the flowers blooming) and we'd say to him

the goldfish is back in the bowl, the flowers are blooming,
all the little superficies seem to have a sheen to them and somewhere

a new *raison d'etre* pulls himself up through the cracks, fake soldier,
you wanted us attentive to the little things and so we were.

Cannibalizing a lecture, sitting still and boiling as the voice face disappears,
one is confronted with some sort of whiteboard or blackboard

and that is the goal as it should be, verticalizing the waistline
each horizon gives us unselfconsciously, like a sleepwalking old

demented old man, then, after six long years, the little man came back again
singing songs he sang across the water (rather unbeautiful songs)

after which this sort of dumb negation would continue with no end.
Well, you said, holding up your pants against the ever-growing waist

in the center of the new world, the face of the new world,
the goldfish is back in the bowl, the flowers are blooming,

we move because we don't much like the music
and the motion of this motion on the horizontal plane resembles black skyscrapers

shoving each other to get what they wanted (a view of the sun)
and necessarily, you add, as some are much taller than others

and we are after all the shorter ones who try to make ourselves look taller
by stepping forward into someone's face.

I must have conceded that this was all true and a massive achievement,
the finest piece of sky philosophy your head had offered

and the oldest river (it makes us look bigger, standing near a river with a history)
put us right and tall against the Chinese lanterns running out along it

like armies in line, or armies in love, all the same color and shouting
thoughts across the river as we still are now.

And what's the point of listening to faceless lectures?
Did he have much to say? What, as it were, did he really have in mind

or whom did he most love stuck there in the room,
but these are only questions, you were quick to remind us, and much as you said

no one would come by to tell us just what we had wanted to know
and the Chinese lights were pretty, not exactly in the way you said they were.

# The Gelding

Soon as you were loosed upon the world you had a rider
and would die before you got him back home.

Whether he would make it walking near death himself
was the only real question on your mind.

You were born standing up, so you slept that way.
You were born beneath the weight of a Renaissance painting

that kept changing color, from black to red to blue.
Breathe in breathe in you said to yourself

and the red lash set you running
though you felt no one on you and felt just as weightless as ever.

But later the air felt like water
and puddles in the way blazed up like agate flesh

and the dear mad life that you'd imagined for yourself
opened out before you into populated places,

the rider lashing you and yelling go back,
whatever that meant to him, wherever that was.

## Repressed Longing

You were the black earth upon which the rock upon which
the church would be built would be built. I was a boy and together
we walked the blank hills to the cliffs and we paused there.
Moher and Galway got into a fight again—Mother is the blank necessity
of all invention, but invention is the mother of necessity.
You had a bloody nose. Nobody told you, instrumental value
pouring from the head. The black river warmed you, but anyway
you feel a bit tired, the moon swings up her big head out of nowhere
and there it is, and there you are, not so much to look at as to hide
by turning away from, or obstructing with this or that sheet of sheet metal at noon.
She lived in the city. Hoping to smoke, I set off her window alarm.
I called up the little Days Inn where she worked. Nobody answered. I sat there
awhile, and Irish men and Irish women walked along the street, and I felt
like a little British criminal a century from the Easter Rising
holding out a basket of eggs. Here, I said, and each one took
just as much as I'd expected, leaving me with change to buy my ferry ride home.

## A Thing on a Wall

Labor began with the breaking of water.
Zeus put on his suit of feathers.

We raised up our augers.
Will what we become have a ring and a wind to compel us?

We raised up our daughters
carefully pinning the broach

over the hem of the garment—
whatever gold we could we gave, whatever charm,

until the pupils had their own hardness.

Leaning on the campanile on the hill

we swim in the womb of the bell,
head like a womb, the night like a hill.

## Violin Playing Herself in a Mirror

Then you had to have a candelabrum for a head
with the flames blown in different directions

so you could mimic the men burning down at the end of the alley
and on down the alley and so on

so that you could keep on with your "going"
though you were not "going" anywhere—

somehow she floats like a pear diorama, horizontal image of a woman or a man
grinding on herself with one limb

sadness that she grinds out so happily,
having given up on playing happy songs

then you had to have a candelabrum for a head
with the flames blown in different directions

burning its image back into the lens of the brother
who threw his coat over the chair like a shadow

and walked off some months later with his shadow intact.
*Did I say so?* No, but you sort of indicated

that the men were at the end of their lives
in a blacked-out valley, and whatever would happen

had happened before in a more perfect way.
Somehow she floats like a pear diorama, horizontal image of a woman or a man

rubbing the rosin all over his bars
like a longarm or another slippery prisoner

trying to open the world in a simple political way—
ibid but this time she says

I am the git pulling fish from the tarn I don't want.
I am the eyeball without any iris.

# Cycle of a Scythe through a Field

Asura put her best face forward—the sun got in line with the earth—
and what you were saying became like a hall, through which the things you would say

in decades to come would crawl slowly, brushing their hands on the walls,
air through a scarred throat and given its voice, only to remark that the scars

seem to resemble a hall with their parallel lines like the lines of a ski
or a skier's wire legs, propelling his white nose back into the powder and saying

I think it's time for chardonnay and oysters in the lodge, the vast little lodge
of our making and becoming and undoing and the rest, but first we must address the
    occasion

with pinstripes and nothing, making up a prison with the chairs,
sitting down to dinner doing nothing to deserve what we have done

or Vishnu swats a housefly from his third arm with a shrug
of his hidden fourth shoulder, holding up a mirror to the creature

and you tell us why you don't believe in deeper sorts of things,
even as you flick the lights another twenty times to ward them off before you rest

or kill the field outside the window with the beasts
bodying their way through the window, or other evil people at your level

with trouble with their heads, and twenty more corrections,
and sipping the wine as you made them, and what you were saying became like a hall.

## Half a Rondo

Morning boy calls to the evening, across the great distance, *bring me a cake,*
and he's sitting on top of himself in a chair on the terrace

wondering why the big city is shrinking as he walks away, or why the lights
describe themselves in fainter color, and it's not clear where they give up and let in
    the night

but without them he can't see at all. The squall says no, but you go out anyway with
    no umbrella,
the city says something in milspeak and puts the long white cigarettes against the sky,

the long black cloves and brown cigarillos you loved as a child, smoking in Paul's shed
and taking a sip of the wine from his father's high cupboard (later he moved out alone)

but right now the sky is a quiet old star-fill that you cannot see,
the gramophone iris is silent and gold where it wilts in a vision beside you

lining as it were your forward progress into something you've achieved,
already finally putting your feet in, the kiddie pool reflected in the big one.

These days the terrace is really a barricade, keeping out the big green hedges
hedged against losing his head, pulling out a note, and clove after clove,

a joint or a spliff, twisting the back of the mind as one twists a balloon, and letting it fly,
putting his habit or stole on, over the dove-tailed vestment, for no one but himself.

So she brings him lemonade and crackers, and several parts of cow he never knew.
She brings him little spices from the market down the road.

## The Equestrian Team

Well, there was this moment, and there was this other, a human-headed bird
gifted with a smaller frame than harpies are, and flying farther

toward the windows and grass, but landing on nothing, your heart as you say
trembles with the violence that it wishes to inflict upon Mark, your ragged ex-lover,
    but you do nothing.

I've been walking up hills. Churches have been walking down through me into hills,
and I am the wise one, I fill myself up, *con brio* as he says, referring, I think, to no one
    in particular—

someone died again and so we shoveled him in, but that was its own all-too-
    conclusive sort of story.
Buses pass, collapsing the distinction between roads, and crossing here you find
    yourself

smaller than you were a time ago, the length of which you measure with a ruler in
    your pocket.
"God I've gone so far in so little," a giant wakes up behind a trebuchet the size of
    his head

and puts a couple nail shavings in it and fires, and the grasses, tall as they are, tall as
    the shadows
of grasses, at some late hour of geometry and cash, present us with nothing we care for.

It's terrible, the big fans lined along the walkway in the big backyard,
we're walking up a hill, and shoveling him in, it's Bob's day and probably John will
    be next

and we'll break down and die, a metonymy, a quick foot, a quick bit of laughing,
and the cable is pulled to the truck and the big man gets in.

But do you want to work here in this industry or don't you? Slowly though the
    metaphor for sin unfolds
in spools of yarn you throw along the sidewalk, spider veins in Mommy's flaky leg, a
    hysterical poet,

Father is back from the army and holding his child—the automatic hospital doors
    then come to a close.
Curtains for centuries. Nobody knows where the one aspirin is that you lost in the
    cabinet.

Lately the swallows evading their names, putting their toes in the water, landing
     in nothing,
taunting the man on the wire, taunting the man at the window, taunting the man
     on the stairs,

halfway up the couple is speaking, the blank son buried in the yard, somewhere
     north of Ferry Creek
or some such city, the red brick building of our lives but as we never really lived
     them—

it takes no discernment to hold up a camera, knowing what will never be the same
again and now, ripped around the corners, trying on the Plymouth and the Boodle's
     and the Hendrick's

and the Five O'Clock Gin, going on with naming things, one name extinguished
     means ten new names
and deliveries made, a pregnant woman walking up the hill, and the slate says hi,
     out of the contrivance

borrowing the brightness of the sun, and is still dim and gray.
You child, you say to yourself, and so feel the same as a child, north of Ferry Creek
     or some such city,

blaming the weather whatever it was for the couches left out in the rain, for
     moving away
out of the valley in New York and into the city, out of the valley in Plymouth and
     into the hills,

out of the shoals and the others and into the cape, out of the mind, and into the
     mind necessarily
speaking and out of the mind and again, and into the mind. But you have a system
     and a friend

and a cornice and a party hat for little Jimmy's birthday, and Chrissy as she lit up
     the town
with just about everything she said, and children on a swing, on a puzzle mat

laid against the grass, which will one day become mud, and probably already has,
but will once again, so it is written, and so it was said in a quieter more lucid way.

## The Academy of St. Martin in the Fields,
## Under the Direction of Sir Neville Marriner

Pieces of rain on the trees or a businessman plucking a reed
from the river with the double stream. Or was it a case

of being there being the stone in the stream, the slick on the stone,
hindering the alternately forward and backward regression and progress—

I'm tired of the motion as it is and as it was:
we went and learned nothing, referring to the reeds,

melismatic singing of a happy child running down the halls,
the center that is not a center, as the Frenchman says

thinking of the mind or Eiffel Tower.
If you stretch up the top of your thought to the top of a tree

you become like the transparent eye you were meant to become,
but all the white film lacks control (it bleeds into the air)

and the songs, so far as they are songs and you can tell us what they are,
are new songs that we've nonetheless extruded

through the same old set of arbitrary instruments
technology was meant to put away, which stayed in our hands, keeping us warm.

# III

## Pithy Reflections of Common Machines

There she was dragging the new world back into the old one,
one street periscoping into another, what do you mean, blinding the men

with how she held her dress above the water, under a parasol,
when the gaunt face of reason promenaded through a cloud

like a gray man, having done nothing with life, brushing aside his gray hair
somewhere where the tile purse becomes a funhouse floor

you carry in this way and hide your money in, and the jewelry rack becomes
the wire-frame blueprint of a scarecrow—whom no crow was stupid

enough to alight on, so finally he took his own life—and she adds
that the man appears in horrible condition: someone's screwed his head onto his neck

and muscle protrudes without thinking from bone
as if it plans to lift a thing or carry forth the body, which has no major error in its legs

and eyes have been inserted in the eyeholes by a hidden hand,
so sometimes we'd sit down in the in-between times

and sometimes we'd walk out and retrace the circle, bedroom to office,
through which a wallet could fit, through which a child

and so much for our loitering, the pomegranate tassel said,
one street becoming another, a gray man who brushes aside his gray hair.

## Two Lungs

Outside the mine, I met a superb lyrebird.
He was bound to a slave and his song was the chain,

wind and glasses clinking in the dark.

Then a Russian girl from the Rathmines
came up and whispered her name, which I have forgotten,

long black hair locking hands with the tail of the bird.

We all carried coal to the roofless breaker up the road
and watched the shadows work

to make the sky-sized meteor.

Pipe in the mouth of the conscript and me with my candle,
the swan in the girl.

# A Russian Dance and Eastern Intermezzo

So they said the staying power of the sun was low—
how it broke us all day long then gave it up

sometimes a blessing, sometimes a man or a woman,
burnishing herself against the corner of the world

and it was current (the thought was) when the other big obstacle
popped its man head up from nowhere

swishing its tail, a sort of manticore in a chimera.
Wait, though—I wanted to tell you (and here

he takes her aside for a moment in front of the door,
romantically blocking her exit).

Your father, his father and his, and his father
told the same stories because they were part of the same train

in which plastic apples replaced real temptations
and a plastic knife sang beyond the observation glass

in the kitchen at the back of the plush car we ate in,
which was just a word for one part of the train.

## Gressorial Waltz

Through the recursion of and how does that
fucking make you feel we reached a cabin

where dark things happened.
Rocs crawled back to their mountainous eggs,

rocks returned to their mountains.
I was an infant then, beautiful, infinite.

Through the recursion of and how does that
fucking make you feel we sleepwalked in

the general direction of stallions,
which I'd often longed to be against a mountain

north of Chicago and close to the lake's
vacant trough, which was likewise endless.

# Blue Kite

So chorus the girls, so chorus the boys—
someone was saying the voice was a vague prerecording

transferred back and forth from wave to tape and tape to wave,
giving the illusion of forgetting us itself

and swaying like the girls, and pumping like the boys though it was neither,
a skyscraper weak in the knees

becoming a geyser or more of a spritz from a can
minus the black glass and metal and water—and so

chorus the girls, so chorus the boys,
moving though it wasn't really moving:

a circuit cannot hang itself, the light's a circuit,
therefore there were two small consolations, brighter than life,

then we found ourselves inside an anthill diorama
and passed the small diversions of the circus (the panther man, the girl with
    the sun in her head)

and headed for the tent we would perform in,
thirty steps north of the hollowed-out river we'd come from.

## At the Day

Where we were playing, where we were loved,
        a body was destroying its body above us

giving us a way to see the vacant faces then
the oval-faced lakes with their grinning

and by the time we noticed, it was raging and bloated
on the verge of speaking up or wrapping us

with what it felt and then you said, as was your wont,
*I am only here a moment passing by the field again,*

*I am only here a moment passing by the field again,*
the motion of which lacked conviction and failed to convince us.

Meanwhile elsewhere and dutifully,
the subjects are filtering out through the doors

back to the outsized pink evening lit up with old myths—
vespers and aspers and all that—holding

on in a real sense to what they believed.
Gorgeous music they were shaking from the harness of the mule

but she herself was laden with the psychic weight of *building*
the place and the hedges which kept out the neighbors.

*Good,* says the good Swiss physician,
spoonfeeding muesli to one of his patients, but what was the dish

his wife had unearthed in the field?
Why was the glacier reduced to a tarn and a large field

through which we hiked to the northernmost tip of the continent?
*I'm tired,* every boy says happily,

yawning up a chorus out of which the mouth flares
like a paper luminaria, framed by the other red of evening.

## Scene with Sheet Lightning

Then an American hymning his hand down a carib,

anhinga at a window on a richer land
or empty space collapsed around a rival with his face,

the walk below lined with narcissuses,
long aisle light in the twilight of long aisle light in the twilight.

## Blues for Norma

We settled ourselves in the sand
and andirons carried the pith of her body back into the evening.

Having not been down the beach in some time.
There was nothing in the way of time.

And we were always late to recognize her prescience,
how it was the death of this or that she said it was

settling herself in the sand and undressing her camouflage.
She always stoked the fire herself

down the whole blank column.
And since we could only imagine the rest,

what it would be like to be with her body,
we tensed up and settled ourselves in the sand.

Boys: it was the thrust of a star through the tongue.
       Girls: it was the hip of the bloom on the pyre.

Boys: it was the heart in the pit.
       Girls: it was my body. It was my mother.

## Coffee with the Flavor of a Ground Cigar

The final thought falls from the biodegradable scaffold
toward the cave where the others, holding their kites, peering up out at the world

and sipping their juice from the vast
canisters we've thrown down in quieter moments, and what does it matter,

it matters not at all or a great deal in fact, as the big voice says,
a ghost stretched between two poles in a field of purple wheat,

a blasé metaphor for guilt and meaning, the sort of derision your father would heap
on your plate with the dull mashed potatoes,

your father sitting there against the window
framed with a frame and two candles, after the war, forming a goal

through which you flicked all your letters and bad origami,
having given up on really working or turning yourself into other things—

the final thought falls from the biodegradable scaffold
toward the cave, where it's cleaner anyway, and drums are played

and people dress without concern for others,
it's a wave, it's a saw, and it's a square again, whatever you said

that's what it was, pointing to the speakers with one hand
and tapping your hip with the other, a small boy in a picture in a picture.

## The Shell and the Crane

The crane put his ear to the shell and the shell put his ear to the crane,
the wave put his ear to the hull and the hull put his ear to the wave

and what you were saying of bodies and bodies, and bodies and bodies,
hit us like a saw against a crystal but illuminated nothing—

Ah, sighs the twilight, I don't know whether it's night or it's morning
that's coming even now across the country in abbreviated form,

under the unreconciled corner of the Afghan rug
is rough matte nothing pressed against the mud earth, but it is a pretty surface.

Not much will help the pink crane in the shape that he's in,
the shell is hard and dead and full of gorgeous rigid culls,

the crane put his ear to the shell and the shell put his ear to the crane,
the wave put his ear to the hull and the hull put his ear to the wave.

## Noble Rider

How would you know that the hollowed-out star is a chain, the bracelet a chain?

Improbably the robin survived, conflated with a sunset in the corner of the mind—
you felt too relaxed, because of the rain, and irises and loose strife

gave the park its ardor and its eau de whatever the marketers said, dreaming
and tossing themselves in the dream, so you would know that the hollowed-out star

is a chain, the bracelet a chain, the place-name a chain and a loose string of islands
anchors the mind now and then as it looks at the water, a vast schooner cloud

with one screw loose, filling up with water as your father says, jester-father
just before dementia in the giddy throes of loving what he was, killing what he is,

shrugging off the hit of what he would become and so on, hill of the profile donkey
flush with the hill. I watered all the flowers with a glass vase painted with flowers.

## Back and Forth between the Map and Living

Mourning Miss Karenina or trying to,
face or an imagined face and train or model train

whistling a thin noise in place of a real one.
That is, did you hold up a hand in your head

and attempt to yell out where you have
no "voice" allotted to you or your hand?

To illustrate this kind of situation, oils and snow,
one throws down a pallet and sleeps off the dream.

Whether the brown vertebrae really circled the world
dotted here and there with all the pennies

the boy day carried up and laid down
and they laid her down again beyond the story of her dying

in the shopworn place she died in
so that she could die again—according to Hirsch

you had to trust her gossamer hair had a "thereness."
You had to put yourself in her little red shoes

and put on her clothes, Gadamer said.
Light has little patience for your talking

shining on the back of the window:
if saying yes would bring back your friends

(they've gone to the bar at the center without you)
you'd say yes, having the smallest ambitions.

# IV

## Stand Again before Your Marble Body

Then I slowly came to understand the aim of the joke:
we who had drawn the red lines on our t-shirts

wouldn't get to play the games we wanted anymore,
the tic-tac-toe would always be a draw, and whatever could

be won was not worth winning, etc., as the drivel waterfall said,
so I took my head out of the baptismal pool and snuck out

with the organ in my stomach like an overblown Scotsman.
I was like a turkey in the middle of the night, surrounded by wives,

and you decided that the tree was your favorite endeavor,
how it tried to be beautiful always

and never to hide what it felt, going so far in the morning
to dress up the seeds that it scattered back into the woods

with the grace and attention of someone's maternal grandmother
with time on her hands, her body an assortment of white

stuck clocks interlocking in a vast tessellation.

## Curves and Intimations of a Great Disease

The larger part of him has dropped out of the race.
It is time to rejoice and drink gin
menacing the room with its distortions

and what a flower says at night painted and hung
about our vanity and motion.
There is time enough for several more songs

or two more songs or just one
but Jim has closed the book again.
I guess the words will have to be our own.

*When he went out to the forest, his mother closed the door and wept.*
*When he went out to the road his mother warned him:*
You would do well to remember

who you are and where you are from
but you never look or listen.
The larger part of him has dropped out of the race

it is time now for rejoicing and more gin
menacing the room with its distortions,
the big heads all lolling like grass in the wind.

*After Virginia I came to this room,*
says the flower slowly to no one.
Jim opens the book to a song about us

written for us to repeat in this room.
Quickly the picture emerges:
bits of black oil and bits of the red,

her left cheek sickled by the moon
and a bit of green oil and blue,
lots of the orange and a fair stretch of still-naked canvas

touched by a line at the bottom a sort of off-pink
unlike a sunset, calling its absence to mind,
a bit of black ink and a bit of red ink

sickling the one vast leg that is a tree,
green and blue ink in dumb touches,
white ink and segments of endlessnesses

touched up with pencil the color of pencil
not unlike a mind, calling final dullnesses to mind
but Jim has closed the book again.

## Meaning in Other Words

The sepia first third was beautiful—slow and assured music halting whenever the hem brushed the wall, because she is in a small room and she's dancing with no one. She slips from her slip into three different boys. What was a city becomes a collection of shacks. And the boys above all love America, a sword in a river. Surely you know about this one. The woman gives it up and says, Don't pretend you know what this is. And they hold it up and scream it is something. She dies or she goes back to living there under the water. She misses the city, the beautiful sepias, low sun a repetend over the field.

# Under the Tree

Suddenly the taciturn myth has convolvulus in it,
        confusing Queen Anne's lace with baby's breath

in a field of white eyes as she says, and not a little softly
        as she floats on.

There was never much trouble
crowning as if for no reason, throwing the curtain, then another one

like this girl in the deepening sequence of dresses
        ascribing the seasons to some human purpose

        in a field of white eyes
with yellow irises, noon repeating himself in a field

like a burden she brushes aside, involving a swell,
giving things whatever names she gives them.

## Emotion Recollected in Bitter Reflection

Reporting that they cried more and the wind looked
meaner than it once had, holding their heads in their hands

and always this butterfly shape,
       a butterflied salmon or open prayer book, their heads in their hands.

A series of apostates filtered through the tunnel,
nothing left to say of what they'd been through

       and you and I anyway, holding our heads in our hands
over our coffee and game of chess

only one of us is interested in playing,
and the moon when the hero and reaper have left

hating and hitting the water
and pulling it up, so far as it can, as if making a garment to wear

and failing again and again. Yet I doubt the reporter
is interested at all in their stories, those others with which it began,

road into a wreck where there were persons
*put away* for a moment whose voices remind us

how much weight and space were there, the relationship between the two
as muddled as ever,

how you could go on wherever you wanted
carrying stones, the gizzard developing, the new tail whipping the stones.

## Godheads I Left on My Lawn

Alexander doesn't shy away from jargon. Alexander doesn't shy away from depth.
The pulley pulls the sun up whenever she says what she says, which she means
    ambiguously

with just as many valences as sunrays on the water, giving it a sort of gold armor
so it can go out with nothing inside it and come back at night to the nothing inside it

as Alexander does, and Alexander doesn't, as Alexander did, and Alexander didn't,
slinky accordion wormhole the sun painted gold, slinky accordion wormhole the moon
    painted white,

I'm delighted to meet you again in the vast chandelier of the city, subtle preposition
with your head strung out along a flowerbed you cannot name the flowers in, feeling
    calm.

They get out the tenor. Alexander doesn't shy away from jargon. Alexander doesn't
shy away from depth. The pulley pulls the sun up whenever she says what she says.

## Fête

They were scheduled for an intimate appearance
in his red front parlor, but they were not there.

This was typical behavior,
the nonet breathing heavily so many leagues away,

a cloud coming into him, the stench of their dresses,
the hue of their hair.

And he knew that the sudden jag of laughter
meant a set was over, in some other bald man's

red front parlor they were finally undressing themselves
in a manner of saying

quick, come with us, we will show you.
And he loved them and he loved them

and he held out his hand and he held out his hand
and the oldest crone kissed the one hand

and the cloud kissed the other,
it didn't matter which or what their names were,

only the crones were worth caring for.
It was like leaving a body

and feeling that you had not been there,
or not long enough for a real conversation.

## Northern Flicker

It takes on this plasticity and bends but might not break,
I'm not sure. She wants me to take what I was

out to the back with the gas can, while the children are sleeping,

and she (another woman) sees it all laid out before her
since it is just one thing, which is what she prefers to think of.

And finally the bird, mimicking the tree enough he *owns it* in a sense
but different enough that he is beyond us—that he can go

just when we find ourselves mixing them up
and his eye is the eye we once mentioned, severed and dropped

because it was used at that point, and stood there as brilliant
and vacuous and moving as a prism.

Lately then the breath is lost.
Every umbrella we gave to the closet resembled a weapon

so what is it doing with them? Why doesn't it rain?

## Walking through a Real Big Garden

Sitting on the porch and smoking Newports was all she and Mom had in common.
That was the end of the novel.
Put her in a hymnal and the paper-thin pages dissolve, leaving song.

Still though I knew there was more to the overall story, the mountain-backed bear
and muscle of so many others—people like we are—scurrying out of the range
of the weapons that the bear had made.

All is best in the best world, and losing oneself is a small loss
(there are after all several pictures, several films, of what you did before the curtain fell
and you emerged minutes later, pretending you had used the time to change)

but the question of having the leftover ham with the leftover rice
stuck to the edge of the frame as a uvula stuck to a wall, hanging in the fleshy
little manner of a slug who has no say in what he is, not very beautiful

but not without his own redeeming virtues.
How often I have thought of it, etc., and hummed the right song with the wrong words
or hummed the wrong song with the wrong words, bringing new meaning

to things I would rather not touch—
thus begins the bad soliloquy, which everyone struggles to end,
in the mouth of the tone-deaf invincible singer, but once again we thought we
      should listen.

Mom hated her boyfriend, Jim, and she herself was angry at Mom
for leaving her father, Ted, for a taller richer man, ad nauseam.
Even the crickets are laying down gently their black violins as a form of surrender

or gesture of peace—let's get along, they say to the lovers in fits of Morse code.
That was the end of the novel.
There rose in its place a new city with towers for eyes, from which someone was watching.

## The Human Career

You always know the sinners by the way they say the title
in another room and long before they say the thing

as if it were some wholly separate floating island.
The marsh gas is quiet tonight, planning out a new

*ignis fatuus* moment, as Billy the redhead says,
and ghosts are on the rampart of the vestige of the edge

of the last civilization she left, a sordid mining town
on the outskirts of a giant coal town at the edge of the water.

You always knew wherever she went
the sinners went too—you who were your own ghost and so

scared the people you were quarantined far from your body
but your spirit was far anyway, as you said,

and the sentence of distinction only ratified the sense
you sort of lacked a groundedness and packed

each morning for the next big hill
your toothbrush, your shoes, your books on the realest phenomena

science had not yet explained, hovering there like the lights
on a camper at midnight, the scarf of the world,

the maps on which the legends were touched with red pen
toward a more perfect myth, and her bliss lips (the image of them)

seemed to suggest you go forward a god
which to be honest was only the wind and a cold

exaggerating your and my differences, a minor catarrh
after which the throat clears and it's nighttime again.

Juniper
Prize
for Poetry

This volume is the 38th recipient of the
Juniper Prize for Poetry, established in 1975
by the University of Massachusetts Press
in collaboration with the UMass Amherst MFA
program for Poets and Writers. The prize is named
in honor of the poet Robert Francis (1901–1987),
who for many years lived in Fort Juniper,
a tiny home of his own construction, in Amherst.

www.umass.edu/umpress